BURNING WATER

BY

Tod Cheney

The Japanese drilled for oil as early as the 7th Century. They called the black substance they mined from the earth

Burning Water.

Introduction

In the year 2031 a pan nationalist terrorist sect attacks the oil production infrastructure in the Gulf of Mexico. CRUD blows eighty-four wells in an unprecedented act of ecological warfare. The explosions mark the beginning of runaway oil spilling into the Gulf of Mexico.

The oil industry lacks the capability to cap the destroyed wells. Marshalling all available equipment, after three years they manage to seal off only twelve wells. Year after year, then decade after decade, millions of gallons a day flow out of the earth into the world's oceans. Natural currents and huge sea storms spawned by climate change disperse the oil to every ocean, every continent. The entombed remains of tens of millions of birds, sea mammals, and fish rim the world's shorelines. Lightning storms ignite the oil, and the oceans burn. The Gulf is no longer navigable through the oil and smoke and fires. After a decade of exhaustive efforts to contain the damage, the world's governments are bankrupt.

As governments continue to disintegrate,

political and social organization revert to medieval models of localized control. A so called Stadium Culture rises around traditional population centers and former professional sports arenas.

Along with it a new class of despots revive methods of cruel and unusual punishment in desperate attempts to control the dwindling populations. Impaling, common in the Middle Ages and used by some Eastern European countries into the Twentieth Century, is the practice of torture and execution by skewering a person on a sharpened post. The despot Blue Cavalry Hat initiates the practice to discourage resistance to Stadium Culture in the rural populations.

Methods of impalement vary. Some practitioners start the stake in the mouth and hammer it down into the chest cavity to exit the body in the pelvic region. The stake can be planted vertically in the ground with the victim head down or hung horizontally on a raised frame. Anal insertion is more common with the stake set vertically. The body descends under its own weight until meeting the ground, the stake exiting somewhere in the upper torso. Other methods include using poles fitted with a stop which arrests the victim's fall after a couple of feet of insertion. Beyond reach of the dog packs that hang around the paling locations, it can take several days to die. Some victims will call out to passersby to pull on their legs so that the stake might run through and finish them and end the suffering. Besides dogs, wolves, rats, wild boar, and vultures populate the paling corridors. Vultures have a taste for eyes and sometimes land on the head while the victim is still alive. The rats climb the poles, and prefer the genitalia of males. Dogs, wolves, and boars must be more patient and wait for bodies to decompose and sink to the ground.

As for the personal interactions of the individuals in the story, the search for meaning and survival, the violence, the underlying struggles for love and relationship, none of this is new under the sun. What is new is the never ending overcast sky. The sun is gone, obscured by fire smoke, off gassing, and chemical reactions. Humans alive in 2084 will never see the sun. If they do somehow survive the cataclysmic events of Burning Water, many generations will live a synthetic and troglodytic existence until the sun shines on earth again.

As the years of global environmental disaster go by the outcome seems obvious to many educated people, but posturing politicians continue to predict and promise solutions, and brand the doomsayers unpatriotic. Theories about how to deal with the spills abound.

One prominent scientist suggests such a huge transfer of oil from the interior of the earth would change the dynamics of orbit and result in an increase of wobble around the poles. An unbalanced earth, he says, will shake itself apart. He is going to be hung for heresy.

Another researcher posits that the oil pooling in the Sargasso Sea will sometime catch fire, and burn so intensely most of the water in the oceans will boil off. The remaining water will be so salty it will not support life, and so corrosive it will erode the continents.

One think tank recommends detonating the world's stockpile of nuclear bombs over the Caribbean, promulgating the theory that the mega-blast will melt the earth's crust to a depth that will seal off the leaking oil wells. A panel of nuclear scientists and geologists predict an 88% chance of success. However, others argue that while the blast might seal off the wells, the amount of nuclear debris and contamination will cause as many problems as the oil.

One pundit notes that such an event would result in some few hundred to a few thousand elites living in underground fortress-palaces. Early in the crisis disaster entrepreneurs started building secret refuges in anticipation of total collapse. Prices for self sustaining units that would support a family run in the billions of dollars. Private security included. It's rumored that a few of these fortresses are stocked with enough food and water to last the occupants for generations.

For the majority of people living on the planet

though, there will be no luxuries. Survival itself will be the luxury and the struggle. Food and clean water will be scarce and supplies guarded by security forces. There will be no cures for the endemic respiratory diseases and cancers affecting the population.

Most people alive are aware they are a species of walking dead. Still, life goes on.

Preface

2031

The research ship Wave monitors hydrocarbon pollution in the Gulf of Mexico. There's nothing remarkable about the operation and no reason for anyone to take notice of the ship's maneuvers. The sailing routes are routine and from outside there's no way to know the radicalized religious sect CRUD crews the vessel. Their mission is to initiate events that will destroy the known world, and then, according to CRUD doctrine, the New Savior will come into the vacuum, and under his dominion a sanitized and devout world will flourish.

A hard rain shrouds the ship ghosting north by northeast over rolling silver seas. Near dawn the helmsman turns east toward the western Atlantic, and slows speed over the bottom to three knots. At sunrise the eight sub captains assemble in the mess. Four women and four men sit down. They share no words, nod greetings, and eat a last breakfast of oatmeal, white toast and salty coffee. Min, the youngest and by far the prettiest, knows the desalinator is on the fritz because it's her responsibility to maintain it. Last week half the ship's crew had diarrhea from the water, but without replacement parts there isn't much she can do. Besides, at this point potable water is moot. She steals a look at Arore. He'd been watching her, but looks away. KORGE would be displeased to learn of liaisons between the crew.

A few hours ago Min and Arore were alone together for the last time. He resents their mission and blames her for his involvement. He is angry and abusive.

If not for you I would be home in my nice house with my dog Instead I am sailing toward death.

Get a life. We live for CRUD not some flea bitten dog.

Lose a life you mean.

You look nice but are cold as steel. As unfeeling too.

He slaps her on the cheek, then punches her in the side of the head.

KORGE enters the mess and begins a speech about CRUD, how the mission today is manifestation of divine will.

You captains are agents of the Savior. You are the privileged ones. In a few hours you will transcend this earth and rise to eternal glory.

Min wishes he'd stop. She glances again at Arore. His lips are thin and purple. He is not attractive, she decides, in these last hours before ascendency. That makes things easier. That, and the fact he hit her.

The Wave lifts to a swell and Min's stomach turns. She has not been seasick on this voyage, but the dull unsettled stomach is with her all the time. She pinches her leg, brings her mind back to the business of instrument checks. She imagines the voyage of her sub toward the target, the visualizations taught all the captains. The others are staring straight ahead into the silence. KORGE has finished and is looking at her. Independent thinking is a lapse and could jeopardize the mission. She hardens her mouth, and KORGE looks away. It is too close to the time. Even KORGE will not question her at this point.

The captains file out of the mess. In less than half an hour the ship's crew seal them into their submarines and begin to check items off the launch list. From now on they will communicate only with the mother ship. Min feels her little sub lifted by the crane, then lowered into the well. She receives the signal it is time and starts the motor. The electric hum comforts her and the propeller spins vibrations through the hull that soothe her body.

An hour into the voyage the trickle running down the inside of the sub amounts to two inches of water in the bottom sloshing forward and back, side to side. So long as the rate of the leak doesn't increase the water won't be a problem. The prop shimmy bothers her more. Grinding metal sounds more substantial by the minute. Target is less than an hour away but the stories of the subs' shabby construction haunt her. It's no secret several subs went down during trials.

When Wave launched Min's sub she settled a course several feet below the surface. Three miles from target the sub begins a slow descent toward the ocean floor. The rate of the leak increases. Five inches of water and rising is ominous and by now she is wet and cold. Still, CRUD's anthem, the last connection to the world that she cannont turn off, plays continuously through the speaker. Then, something strange. A muffled voice intrudes on the anthem. Min cocks her head trying to make it out.

Then, recognition. She recoils with embarrassment. It is Arore, she'd know him. He is crying, sniffling. Somehow he is transmitting from his sub to the rest of the fleet. How can this man broadcast his cowardice over a loudspeaker. He is crying, afraid of his death.

Shut up you coward. Shut up.

Suddenly the sub lurches left with a violent jolt.

9

Min's head cracks on the pipes. The water rolls up and splashes over her. Another blast spins the sub like a bath toy. A red cloud spreads in the water, and when she touches the side of her head her fingers come off sticky. One of the subs has detonated early. Or maybe it was part of the plan that KORGE had not shared. That would be like him.

She holds her hand to her head and waits for her sub to even out after the explosion. The leaks are worse. A fine spray shoots sideways in front of her face. A buzzer sounds. The signal the sub is approaching target, and it's time for human piloting to take over control. There is the wellhead, a thick pipe encrusted with orange scale. She can make out the dozen bolts clamping down the cap. The second level buzzer sounds shriller and louder. This is the final alarm, the fail safe alarm, the message relaying to Wave she is over target. The intense whistle drowns the anthem still coursing through the speakers, and she clamps her hands over her ears. Her own tears drip into the sloshing seawater. Farewell Arore, farewell lover.

At the same time Min and her comrades drive their submarines toward the deadly rendezvous with the Gulf oil wells, CRUD cells carry out a companion event at the Athabascan Tar Sands in Alberta.

For fifty years Canada has extracted oil from

surface mines and constructed tailings ponds filled with bituminous waste covering tens of thousands of acres. So toxic and powerful are the emissions from this landscape they are detectable on the East coast of North America and beyond. CRUD attacks the oil saturated landscape with drones carrying incendiary bombs.

A week later when governments finally acknowledge the severity and scope of the disaster one analyst predicts the fires would burn for a hundred years, but Canadian and American planes dropping millions of gallons of flame retardants quell the flames in six months. However, the chemicals used to quell the flames are gasified and projected by the extreme heat high into the atmosphere where they combine with existing hydrocarbons and make the most noxious chemical stew. Billions more gallons of burning water flow through breaches in the retention pond berms into the Mackenzie River, drift downstream to the Arctic Ocean, and in time disperse to the world's oceans.

2084

Rain slams the metal roof and wakes Bird into a dark wet world. The runoff splashes onto the ground a few feet from where he lays on a shred of tarp. A rivulet breaks out of a puddle and moves toward him in crooked fits. More deluge. The kind of rain that used to come on a blue moon but is now routine. He tucks the tarp into his body. The rain smells of oil, and even in this shadow light weird rainbows shimmer in the puddle. The rain will hold daylight back longer than usual. He suppresses the rasp in his throat and squeezes his eyes shut. He whistles a few unconnected notes. Used to be he could carry a tune. Now notes drift single file into the forest.

Later, how much later, rotten muffler growl and diesel backfires wake him again. Condensation falling from the underside of the metal roof placks the tarp. The low roof of some farm building remains. Chicken coop, pig sty. A tangle of rusted barbed wire bunched against one side of the shelter. Litter in the wire. The arm of a red plaid shirt, a woman's handkerchief ripped. Faded Bud Light and PBR cans. If this is an old farm maybe there's food. The engines idle out of sight down the hill. Diesel rattling, and mens' voices calling back and forth along the road.

Bird rolls out from under the roof. He stands alongside sumac and bamboo and raspberry thrusting green out of a blackened pile of rubble. A country road, two worn tracks with a grassy middle, leads uphill past the sty one way, and down to the main road where the trucks are stopped the other. Bird's stomach rumbles. He wants to search for the garden, something edible. Asparagus might linger, or garlic. A fruit tree. Instead he creeps toward the crest of the hill for a look at the road. On hands and knees through overgrown field. Generations of blackberry vine and old thorns tear his clothes. The greasy soot soaks him.

Eight disheveled men stand blackly in the road. A ninth man swarms into the waist high scrub waving his arms like a swimmer. Their helmets shine like smooth wet rocks. They are all big men, survivors. You seldom see a small man anymore. Bird watches the ninth man. He looks to be on his own, ranges around swinging his arms, eyes furtive. One of the men coughs into his hand, looks, then holds the blood up for the rest to see. Several of the men laugh and make derogatory gestures.

Movement on the hillside. A helmet bobs in the

foliage, moves uphill toward Bird. He lowers his head. The man comes on, and the men in the road holler.

Come on Earp, come on.

The man turns and shouts something back. The rain in his voice. It looks to Bird like the men intend to leave the man on the hill behind. The man drops his pants and squats. He is close enough Bird can see a blur of purple birthmark on his backside. The squatter curses the men in the road. They climb back into the vehicles, look up the hill and laugh. One lifts a rifle out of the truck, walks to the side of the road. Raises the gun to his shoulder, and settles his right eye to the scope.

Bird watches the beginning of the man's movement. A flare at the rifle muzzle and a bullet whines overhead. The squatting man falls over and curses.

Fuck you assholes.

Down on the road the front vehicle pulls away. The second truck lurches into gear. The man with the rifle stays at the side of the road. The man on the hill stands, pulls up his pants and starts running uphill toward Bird.

His face is gray and rough with old acne. A

scar slants across the forehead. The mouth is just plain mean. The climb challenges him and he coughs into his hand.

What the hell, he says, pulling up when he sees Bird.

Then his face explodes. The rifle booms and a plume of teeth, bone and blood gore spray Bird in the face. He flicks a piece of jaw with tooth attached from the back of his hand. Laughter and jeering rise from the road. The big diesels rev, clatter, and grind, begin to move away. The pitter patter of oily rain fills in the country as the engine throbs subside. Already flies circle and light on the dead man.

Bird whistles a few odd notes, stands up and shoulders his pack. His hunger wells up but the idea repels him. He'd rather have asparagus, but in the aftermath of American exceptionalism it is hard to find living vegetables. He curses Christian obeisance, the failure to live a genuine life. Instead the fear of otherness, childish deceptions, the fear and excuse of God. He turns his back on the dead man. That's not much of a eulogy. At least there are animals enough to effect a burial.

He surveys the scruffy ruins of the farm. Sumac,

bamboo, a few birch grow out of the charcoal footprints of the buildings. On a blistered tractor still hitched to a manure spreader smoky swatches of green paint cling to the metal.

Jesus, a John Deere.

A cast iron hand pump stands in a granite slab in the dooryard. He tries the handle, is surprised the pump holds a prime and with a few strokes a cold clear stream splashes onto the stone. He leans into the spout and laps the water like a dog. A scrape in the gravel road. Fifty feet away the man shot dead on the hill walks toward him.

The man is naked and carries his pants folded over his right arm. The lower half of his face is a red pulp, his torso a delta of blood running down to his pelvis where the penis stands erect. Blood bubbles simmer in the maw of destroyed face. He shuffles a few more steps, pitches forward full out on the ground. Several small photographs spill out of a shirt pocket. Bird breathes, purses his lips to whistle.

Fuck you, says a voice at his back. A shovel handle cracks the back of Bird's skull and he sinks.

Fuck you, says the voice again. Cold water on his

face.

He wipes the water from his eyes. Two mud crusted leather boots on the ground near his head.

Fuck you, I said, a female voice. As if fuck you was some kind of order.

The boots take two steps backwards. He looks up in time to see one of the boots swing into his stomach. The Woman wears only a ripped shirt tied around her waist. Scratches and dried blood cover most of her body.

Take off your clothes and walk away. Leave the tarp and the rest.

He rolls onto his side trying to think, make words into actions if he can. Props himself on an elbow.

Look again and you're dead, she says. And don't talk neither. Take off the clothes now. Bird struggles to get his knees under him.

Keep it on the ground. Take'm off right there. He leans into the ground and vomits. He slides his pants off. Then pulls two shirts over his head.

Underwear too. They slip down, the elastic gone.

He pushes them away with his right big toe.

He avoids eye contact. Crawls off the tarp into a bed of oily leaf mulch. The muck oozes between his fingers and toes. The Woman drags the tarp ten feet away then rushes back with the shovel handle and swings at his head again. Bird ducks and this time she misses. He starts to get to his knees when she runs in from behind and kicks him between the legs.

Can't take chances.

He sleeps, muffled in his beaten body. Time is an empty perch on a barren strand. Sleeps. After some long while he cannot measure he begins an effort to stand up. Naked. The bitch gone with his clothes. He grabs hold of a small birch tree and loosens oily ploks of water. The sky flinches. Somewhere up above the sun sparks the oil in the atmosphere and sets off thunder. He paddy cakes to the water pump and strokes the handle. Using gingerous motion rinses the violence from his body.

He leans under the spout and drinks, pees while he's drinking. Bloody urine dribbles between his toes. He wobbles toward the dead man lying near the edge of the brambly field. The man's clothes are there wrapping his arm, and still in death the erection. There's a name for that isn't there? Priapic it's called, after a Greek fellow. Didn't know you could be priapical and dead. At least I hope he is dead. Of all things, photographs lying on the ground. A woman. Wife, good looking, sitting in a white convertible. Three kids. Dog. That looks like the dead man there, hard to tell. Bird picks them up and looks closer. They are wrinkled and have been wet. Now there is blood on them. Bird wipes them on the grass and puts them back in the pocket.

He lifts the clothes from the man's folded arm. Flies loop around the face. Flecks of red lint cling to the seams of the inside out pockets. Bird dresses in the dead man's clothes and shuffles around the farmstead. He trudges up the old wagon trail and emerges on an outcrop of ledge with a view of the country. In the east looms the mass of Grendal, the Stadium that controls this part of the country. He eases down onto a grassy place and tries to think what to do. He takes the pictures out of the pocket and looks at them. Puts them back. Takes them out. Tries to think what to do.

* * * *

Paling stakes set along roadsides extend out from the Stadium for miles. Designated paling crews in specially adapted trucks patrol the roads in widening circles around the stadium.

When Rena started driving Truck 2 a year ago, Hudj, her supervisor, predicted she'd last a couple of months and today she wonders if she isn't coming up against her limit. Seventy odd paling stakes planted by Truck 1 stretch along the road for half a mile and those are only the ones she can see. The Stadium is five miles up the Avenue, and the palings go all the way.

She wants to look away from the procedure in front of the windshield but she knows Grege is watching her, and that he would seize a chance to out her for his advancement. She poses a calm, engaged expression and watches the tenders struggling with a large tattooed woman. The circle clamps that bind and spread the legs are too small to contain her fat thighs. The tenders are trying to move the clamps lower so they can pick her up closer to her knees.

This could get messy, says Grege.

She almost says they are all messy, but catches herself.

Not many like her left.

A good 250 if she's 100. She'll go fast.

How many are left back there, asks Rena. She could look herself, but keeping up a conversation with Grege is a good idea. Like most survivors he's simple and doesn't think much.

Seven, he says, craning his neck.

Rena feels his sour breath wash over her as he turns. She wonders if Grege has always smelled bad, or if it's his decaying lungs.

Seven. All women. I wonder why?

You know why, she says, punching his arm.

Grege laughs. He smiles toward Rena but she looks away. Nothing there she wants to encourage. The bucket lift bobs up and down in front of the truck. The fat woman is suspended now and the lead tender steers her toward the point of the stake. The tenders pause to adjust their headsets. When she is close enough the second tender grabs hold of the stake and guides it between her spread eagled legs. The woman drops a few inches, then the second tender gives thumbs down and the gantry lets go. In a second the fat woman slides down three feet.

Rena watches the arms and legs go rigid. The

tenders laugh at the woman's weight. Her slide down the stake slows. Blood streams down the pole. A bulge appears at her throat, then the point sticks out the side of her neck and thrusts the head aside. The fat woman loses consciousness.

I'll say she hangs up at ten feet, says Grege. There's an ongoing contest among the crew, betting where a body will stop its drop.

Six feet, says Rena. Suddenly the fat woman jerks back to consciousness, flails her arms and legs and sprays blood across the windshield.

Oh shit, says Rena, and she flicks the wipers on and holds down the washer until the red washes away.

Fuck her, says Grege. By the time the wipers stop the victim has sunk out of view. The bloody shaft sways in front of them.

She went fast, says Grege. They both stand up off the seat to see the woman on the ground. She looks to be kneeling, the stake holding her torso erect. The shaft emerging below her left ear.

Miscalculation on that one, says Grege.

Yeah I guess. Rena sits down. The tenders ready the gantry for the next prisoner.

* * * *

Bird sits on the ledge and surveys the valley stretching toward the Stadium. Rampart fires flicker in the gloam. He sips well water from a dented beer can. The ragged cadences of the anthem bands rise and fall over the landscape. He muses on the bands' particular brand of torture. Nationalism and its propaganda partner, patriotism, bind individual will to the obeisance of the state. Once individuals resign their freedom, they adhere to the illusion they are fighting for freedom. He picks up a stick, snaps it into smaller and smaller pieces.

He decides for want of anything better to follow the road toward the Stadium. With vigilance he can avoid patrols and make better time than trudging the unmarked roads of the backcountry. Besides, those are just as dangerous as the main roads used mostly by the Stadium patrols driving loud diesel trucks easy to stay clear of. He can see the rows of palings, looking in the distance like some kind of fence.

Hunger gnaws, and the countryside feels empty.

Even if he could move well enough to catch something. A chicken maybe, or sheep. He sees nothing. A couple of songbirds. Flitty shadows. A weary hopelessness descends, and he walks slower. After several hours he leaves the road for a grove of old growth white pine and lays down on a little rise of almost dry ground.

Snatches of anthem band drift on the oily air. The one dimensional and repetitive anthem music is the lifeblood of Stadium Culture, and the preferential treatment given band members is common knowledge. The elite bands enjoy their own barracks with hot water and catered dining room. The guarantee of food and housing inspires people who never played an instrument to take up the trumpet and the flugelhorn, the bass and snare drums.

The duty is rigorous. Besides marching duty at the ramparts, each band is required to tour the outlying regions under Stadium control once a week on the back of a flatbed truck. Coming and going along the Avenue of Palings.

A throb of clattering diesels begins far away and moves closer. Spare parts and the people who know how to work on the old engines are ever scarcer. The engines rev up and idle down in erratic pulses. Bird takes stock in the lay of the land, decides to wait out the trucks' passing. In ten minutes two trucks rumble past. They are gray and rusty and drag black clouds of exhaust. Both have telescoping cranes mounted on the back, the first carries a rack full of sharpened poles. A small anthem band standing and playing in the long bed of an ancient Ford F150 brings up the rear. He covers his ears when they pass.

You know they arrest people for less.

He starts at the voice, and his carelessness. The Woman stands ten feet away, hands gripping the shovel handle.

Ah it's you. I'm a generous man generally. I don't think I'll kill you which is pretty forgiving by my book. Most guys would fuck your ass and cook it over a fire.

She stares at him.

I had no choice.

No? I can think of a few.

You're not a woman.

I hear that all the time.

Yeah. How many times have you been raped?

Bird scrapes the ground with his foot.

None.

You just answered your question.

A crow glides over the ground without making a shadow. The crow is his own shadow.

I have a place near here, she says.

What kind of place?

She leans forward and looks at her leg through the hole in her pants. His pants.

A cabin.

A cabin?

Of sorts. There's food there.

Anyone else know about this cabin.

No. It's a few miles.

Why me? You might as soon killed me.

We got off to a bad start.

Really.

Bird lags, sore. She stops, turns, waits. An hour passes and neither speaks. He begins to think not unkindly toward her. The band sounds faint and far off through the woods.

He almost walks by the cabin. It's a rough affair of vertical logs leaning into a cliff. Willowy smoke exits an opening and slides along the face of dripping rock. A dirty piece of canvass hangs across one end of the shelter. Not something most people would call a cabin.

Inside there is a sound of scraping metal. He pushes the canvass aside and walks in. The Woman tends an iron frying pan over a little tin stove. Stirs something meaty with a spoon.

Out of a can, but it's real meat.

A Griswold #8.

The Woman smiles, sprinkles something from a

bottle into the pan.

It's hard to trust anyone. Could be I overreacted back there. You know Griswolds.

A 7, 9, 11, and 13, at one time.

This one was my grandmother's.

Something left. More than I have.

There's a narrow cot made of logs held together with rope and wire. A sleeping bag rolled and tied with string at the foot. A few tin cans and glass bottles stand in a wooden box nailed to the logs.

Sit, she says. Carries the frying pan to the table and scrapes the food onto a white china plate. She ladles water out of a bucket and puts a small pot on the stove. Opens the stove door and pushes a handful of sticks into the firebox.

Tea fire, she says. Then sits on the bed and watches him eat.

This is good.

An old Dinty Moore recipe passed down from

my grandmother. Not the Griswold Granny.

The rest is yours, he says and stands up.

Never mind that. You finish. The tea and biscuits will do me.

You do all this yourself, he waves the fork around to take in the cabin.

Umhmm.

How far are we from a road.

Mile maybe. To a dead end dirt road. Comes in off the Avenue.

You been along the Avenue?

Stove needs more wood. He kneels and pushes a handful of broken branches inside. A sudden sea of domesticity.

Have you?

What do you think?

It wasn't really a question.

After eating he goes outside to relieve himself. Picks his way through boulders following a copse of pine. Pulls down his zipper and aims between two rocks. It is getting dark and he feels sleepy. His body aches all over. His stream splatters on something not a rock and Bird tenses when he recognizes a skull. When he's zipped up he pokes a stick in an eye socket and lifts the skull out of the rocks. You find bones everywhere now. Corpses don't get buried but torn, eaten, dispersed. A kind of environmental justice to that end, human flesh joining the scheme of things.

And how is your day going, he asks the skull. Then sets it down on a rock.

A better view from there my friend. Who you might be, though you be dead. And a long time of it by your pallid color and empty sockets so long unseeing. The sourness you have tasted and I have not. Not yet. Though I am walking dead. We are all the walking dead. The blood leaking from our lungs. Our breath the putrid air of old men. You are not the bleached skull of the laboratory, but moldy and algae pocked.

Bird runs a hand through his hair.

At least I have hair, which is more than this

fellow has. Ah. In this interval dark is falling. Now is dark my friend, now is light. Dark will be the longer tenure. But wait. What are these arcs of light. Stars! Wondrous stars! How long since I seen the stars? How is it humans never had a plan, but just did the next thing dumb as any animal. That's how we came to lose the stars. Even now this front of inky cloud, brow of soot and oily air stubbing in from the south. Is this the stellar window closing for the last time? Oil still flowing out of the ocean floor.

He sinks as lead in the ocean. Collapses into exhausted sleep on a sea of pine needles.

Oh Ahab, This Indeterminate Time.

Somewhere an anthem band drones. An indistinct diesel clatter. Woman says the road is not far. The hunger is back.

He rubs his shoulder working feeling back into it when movement makes him freeze. A tall man dressed in black camo makes his way along the path. His helmet and poncho shine with oil. He coughs, breathes in thick gulps. Strokes his black beard with meaty hands creased with black lines. He stops, holds a thumb to the right nostril, leans over and blows a spray of red goo onto the ground. He switches to the left side and blows red green phlegm on the rocks. He coughs into his right hand and looks again. His left forefinger goes up the left side and comes out bloody. After an inspection the man puts his finger into his mouth sucks and swallows. A raspy exhale and belch the oaf extends in practiced soliloquy. He fumbles a small glass bottle out of a breast pocket, twists off the top and tips two small pink pills into the palm of his hand. He throws the pills into the back of his mouth and gulps like a fish.

The camo man pulls a finger out of his nose and unzips his pants. A banana sized penis spills out. He points at the ground and urinates. His stream a pinky chartreuse. Stadium populations suffer an epidemic of kidney disease, and blood in the urine is ubiquitous. Bird watches the stream subside. Instead of closing up he undoes his belt, lets his pants fall, and starts to stroke. The raspy breaths quicken. The fat hairy hams are a blotchy pink pocked with hair follicles. After a minute of furious stroking a blur of marbly cum arcs into the cusp of his left hand. He claps it to his mouth. His voice slurs.

Drostne cherg masdi. Cherken doisten braquen up moiri.

He sashays one leg forward, bending at the waist while extending his right arm.

Buerre au as gesten melaeni. Heleni abrostunken fesite.

He pushes his penis back in his pants licks the fingers on his right hand and rubs his hands together.

Begoast au Heleni jubareste. Ha ha jubareste de corekese ha ha.

And then, pawing his thatch of black beard, patting his stomach, he lumbers off in the direction of the Woman's hutch.

Bird watches the shuffling man disappear in the piney woods. He imagines the camo clad clod coming upon the Woman's hutch. Entering. He stands indecision companionably. Takes a step to follow, pauses. Turns back. There is decency and there is survival. He quits each one. As a boy he kissed the foamy lips of the sea, then grew into the man sick with the tragedy of mountain, river, sky, and sea. Vested in the forlornness of human occupation. For each their own, in this day and age.

The Woman cleans up after the meal. There is not much to do because there is not much. But still, one takes care. She heats some water on the dying fire.

A little bit for her face, and some to wipe off the plate. Nothing gets clean the way things used to. Sweep the floor. She likes the way the broom makes lines in the sandy soil, the pattern of it before her footprints. A remnant of the mundane. Who thought that would be missed? She touches the cans on the shelf. Lines them up. There are no labels to turn outward, but there is the seam on the can to align. The folds on the bedding to smooth. There's Bird scratching outside. What men find to do in the world. Their bent for disassembly. Predilection for manipulation, that is the definition of the male species. But shit, it's not Bird but some idiot slob in black camo.

Bird follows sounds through the maze of forest roads. Amazing sounds. The song of a stream that emerges whole from the underworld. Old twitch roads when the trees were a forest. The intrusion of horn and engine. He needs to see things for himself. The progress of impaling. Why would he do that? Why not go the other way? There is the sweet song of a wayward warbler.

The incessant rampart fires. The diesels' grinding reverberations through the valleys. The pistons' echoes. Waiting for the cataclysm, everything is an echo of what has come before. Oil dripping out of the sky. Now here is a road. An anthem band on a flatbed truck leading a paling crew, the pole setter, and the personnel truck. The personnel truck stocked with prisoners.

Bird waits. The convoy passes. When he starts to stand three black helmeted camo men appear on the hill across the road. Like most Stadium mercenaries they are obese from the carbohydrate and sugar diet. He feels the hunger and imagines the contents of their backpacks. They laugh and stagger along with sloppy, splayfooted gaits.

One man against three men is not good odds, but he lays and watches anyway. They take a break beside the road. One pulls a bottle from a pack and twists off the cap. They pass the bottle around, light cigarettes.

Bird watches. One man finishes a bottle and throws it into the woods. A few minutes later they throw a second bottle against a rock. The banter slurs and one man turns on his side, rests his head on his crooked arm. In a few minutes the sounds of three men snoring drift up the hill. He makes up his mind to approach when several buckskin clad figures appear out of the foliage on the hillside above the sleeping men and move toward them. Bird shrinks from the glint of long knives.

The unconscious men never wake up. The knives

arc up and down three, four times. Errant blood. The buckskins rifle the pockets, gather the backpacks and the weapons, and withdraw into the trees where they had come from. It was over in two minutes. Bird breathes his fortunes. He waits half an hour then creeps down to the scene. Dark blood stains the ground. He hiccups and walks by. That's it. Seriously. He touches the pictures in his shirt pocket, and whistles a few notes.

He walks the roadside until he is too tired to go further. He crawls into a thick wood on hands and knees until he can't see the road and lies down. He dreams of a primordial ape raping a woman in a stone hut. Men with knives in their chests stand around in a circle watching and doing nothing.

He wakes up knowing he'll go back. What he should have done yesterday.

He loses his way. The tangle of roads. North and south upside down. Earth wobbling. The continents drifting on the lithosphere like crackers on soup. No wonder. No sun shines. The oiled sky and the landscape unfamiliar.

Here is a meadow. A strange pile of steaming dung three feet tall. And a rowdy hoard of red beetles scuttling in and out of a hole at the bottom. A cloud of flies hovering. The cloning clock has ticked some unexpected tocks. This atonement for past extinctions comes with surprises. Apparently a kinship with rats. Imagine mammoths reproducing and adapting at the rate of rats. Thank science for the cahoots of rats and mammoths. Broken bones bright in the dung piles.

A brute sweeping twelve foot tusks leads the herd into the misty meadow. The creatures blunder here and there. Hook their tusks under the low lying branches and pull trees out of the ground. A thousand acres plowed up and the ground quaking. The mammoths merge with the earthquakes, toss the uprooted trees with their tusks. A gray rain falls on the gray herd. A yearling breaks away and heads toward Bird. Others veer behind him. The near sighted animals kick the dung piles, spraying clots of black gunk. Ivory tusks blurr by in the oily mists. An avalanche of fetid breath. Bird runs toward the loom of cliffs. The beasts homing in on the aberrant in the meadow. He imagines death by tusk.

A couple of crushed beer cans, then another. Rusted bed springs leaning on the cliff. An opening in the rock, and he ducks inside. A few feet further and the cave scales down enough to leave the mammoths behind.

The creatures scythe their tusks on the cliff face and loose rocks clatter down. They pace and bleat. Their shaggy hides matted with oil. The lead brute inserts one tusk into the cave and rakes the walls, loosening rocks that crash to the floor and spread clouds of dust. Bird relaxes, continues deeper into the cave. Light filters down from above. Water drips. The cave widens out into a large cavern. A place occupied by humans for some time by the look of things. Refugees from Stadium Culture.

Here are a couple of moldy sofas. Frayed Afgans. Flat screen tv on a wooden cable spool. Still plugged into a Honda generator. Empty gas cans. National Geographics puffed up but still yellow. Carved into the top of a picnic table: caves suck, life is warm beer, guns are cool. Back in a corner a pile of Budweiser Lite cans reaches almost to the ceiling. Graffiti sprayed with pink paint. Larry's dick is a toothpick. Lick an oily dick.

It takes lots of detail to make a civilization.

Water plinks on the Budweiser cans. Impale, Exhale, Expire, Right and Rong are Relativity. One might laugh if off but for the bones. Mouldering maggot remains melting into the upholstery. Rank smell of mushrooms, stale beer, old sex. A cast iron pot hangs over a fire pit flecked with aluminum foil. Burned tin cans. Shards of bone. Scraps of electric wire. Cloven footprints in the ashes. Long red tresses lap the scapulas on the black recliner. An Irish beauty once upon a time. A leathery patch of left nipple hanging like a withered leaf.

More trash at the back of the cave. Wet cardboard. Tires. We are a nation of worn, discarded tires. Plastic Adirondack chairs and programs from the fairs. Mining landfills is something like propitious. Maybe delicious. Food of the future. Life repurposed. Reprocessed. Reconstituted. Reconditioned. Reconnoitered. Repelled. Renovated and Regurgitated. Repulsive.

No excuses here, not the wrong story. This is American inventory. The legacy of American exceptionalists who binged on oil for a hundred years. Who built shitty soulless houses for storing consumer junk on it's way to the landfills. Inside the houses they gorge on crappy food, laze on lazy boys, and grow obese. We are the self made battalions of the spiritually impoverished.

Outside the cave the mammoths rake their tusks against the cliffs. No exit. Bird speaks.

There must be some way out of here, said the joker to the thief. Is there nothing left to lose? Am I losing my mind? Absolutely. That would be the last thing to lose. That's where we went wrong, you can trace it to the rise of absolutely, because nothing is, but we say so. Now listen, when I was a young man, when there was relativity because Einstein said so, and before you know it we have the Sea Fires. It's all Jesus' fault. Jesus and Einstein, now there's a dynamic duo. What were they thinking? How did they let this happen? It's all Jesus' fault. I only wanted to be saved and look where we're at. What's this stench? Here's the latrine, an open book as it were. Aren't we the curators of defilement.

He crabs along the wall hoping not to fall. Something greasy on the floor, another kind of spore. Dark and greasy. But a glimmer. A glimmer as the passageway curves into daylight. A back door. Who doesn't like a back door? Sing the blues and enter the back door. Foliage, boulders, emergence on the side of a cliff. A view of the country while staying concealed, always good to be concealed. Wonder what killed those lazy boy corpses? Can't tell now and the coroner had a coronary. Not that it matters. Why obsess over cause of death?

There's the anthem music, like a drip, drip, drip on the brain. Designed to make you insane.

I think I need a gun. Maybe several. Everybody else has a gun, why shouldn't I. If I had a gun I could take care of myself. Shoot something, someone. Someone

I don't like. Oh lord, I been looking all of my life, and now the world's on fire. The world is burning, the world is burning.

Quit the country and take the guns. That's it. We are the vacuous, not miraculous or exceptional, unless we carry our pistoleros. Empty spirits shouting slogans. All my life we have bombed shot burned I mean kill kill kill men women and children at will. Collateral damage for security. We use red blood to write the balance sheets. All my life all my life killing. Men, women, and children in Vietnam, Cambodia, Laos, Latin America, Iran, Iraq, Libya, Afghanistan, Lebanon, Kent State, Philadelphia, Los Angeles, Chicago, Ferguson, Baltimore, you name it, all my life. Time to get some guns. Play patriot, and head someone off at the pass.

Please do not understate the obvious, Mr Jones. No more Walt Disney reruns. It's all real now, the endings are real. The Great Sea fires. Expires. A stash of oxycodone. Killing each other doesn't cost the government anything. Bring it on home, the killing home, what did we expect?

Now, now comes the anthem, drip, drip drip on my brain. Drifting here. Rooting out the illusion of progress, or is it the progress of illusion? Two hundred years of scammed dream. Imagine. A token does not get you a ride on democracy. A closet Oligarchy. Not quite Monarchy.

Here is the road. Everything is going to be all right. I'm not lost, but back on track. I was here some time ago. I am getting my bearings. Yes, I'm back I'm sure of it. It's good to be b b back J J Jack. Drip, drip, drip.

Maybe the Woman is cooking something. Six sense knows I'm coming and is cooking for me. How is it I am losing my mind? Where did I put myself? Maybe she cooks a nice lamb stew in her Griswold Number 9. There is no lamb but maybe she cooks it anyway. Isn't that arrogant of me. Here is the trail and here is the cliff and here is where I slept and the oaf came by. Here is the smoke coming out of the roof. Here is the fine ≦ frizzle of oil. Here is the blood on my hands.

And singing inside the hut. Who's singing? No aria for the ages surely.

What the hell, pulls the tarp aside. Who? The camo clad snotty oaf sitting where he sat before. What the hell did he expect? So who the hell are you? A fat woman laughing out an aria before the stove. It's all another language. Stirring something in the Woman's frying pan. The man with his cock in his hand doesn't he ever put it down. The fat woman disdainful, not an inventory gainful, she. Unimpressed. Stirring. Aromatic. Something fleshy in the pan. And there is the Woman half naked on the floor. Balltied. Rag in her mouth. The oaf turns toward Bird and starts to stand up. The fat woman sees him too. Where the hell did she come from. Seems like there is always a fat lady somewhere. The oaf tugs on his zipper. Both mouths open. The ax leans against the cliff.

Bird severs the big man's right arm with the first swing of the ax. During the pause the big man takes to consider his dangling forearm, Bird cleaves the skull, buries the blade down between the ears. The big man drops onto the fat woman's feet. Blood fucking everywhere. She falls backward onto the stove and collapses it. Screams, hair in flames, burning blood.

Bird crosses the hovel and kneels beside the trussed Woman. The cords are knotted so tight he can't undo them. He goes back for the ax. He covers her with a blanket.

Can you walk?

Carry me.

The ground trembles when he picks her up and

lays her over his shoulder and staggers outside. Stones clatter off the cliff onto the log walls. The fat woman moans, the man is stone cold dead and burning. Bird carries the Woman away until the earthquake bends him to one knee.

The cabin collapses in slow motion. A chaos of stone, logs, fire, flesh. He gets far enough away and lowers her onto smooth ground. Tucks the blankets. The earth stutters with after tremors.

What took you so long?

Can you walk?

My shoes were over by the bed. Go get them.

Bird walks back and pulls away some of the logs.

That's lucky, he says pulling a pair of black boots from the rubble.

I don't feel lucky, she says.

The ground pushes them one way, pauses, jerks back. Bird feels his neck kink.

Could be the big one.

They've been saying that for a hundred years.

More likely now.

It's making a lot of smoke.

We should go.

Where?

There must be somewhere to go.

Not that I know of.

Maybe an island. Somewhere beyond the crazy stadiums.

What do you mean?

I mean someplace sane.

I doubt it. I liked the axe buried in that animal's skull. Thank you.

You're welcome.

She gets to her feet, sways. Bird extends an arm

she ignores. They start to walk.

The stiffness is going away, but you're going the wrong way.

She rubs her wrists. The tremors spring tree roots out of the ground. Bird watches the ground rolling like an ocean.

There are some camps on a pond along up in here. We can go there and rest.

You're from here?

Sometimes.

The road rises and falls through the hills, narrows and turns rougher. From the hilltops the Stadium is visible in the distance. Tendrils of black smoke rise from the perimeter walls.

It's nice to be clear of those goddam bands. Bird spits.

Why did you come back?

A driveway curves off and descends through the cedars. A name carved into a board hanging by one nail says Murphy's.

Not here, she says.

The next driveway sign says Mitch and Peg. They walk a hundred yards to the cabin. A pine tree has fallen through the roof.

Critters been there a long time. Water too.

He turns around and looks across the pond. A cliff rises out of the water. The wooded hills above dark.

There's a place, she says, pointing a crooked finger. There is a porch railing, a low roofline gloomy in a stand of old growth hemlock.

Doesn't look like there's a road to that one, he says.

No, you get there by boat.

They walk behind the broken camp to the shore.

Every camp's got a canoe.

What the hell? he says lifting the gunwale of a wooden canoe. This is an old Charles River. A beavertail paddle falls on the ground.

No life preservers.

It's too late for life preservers.

He paddles from the back seat. She sits on the floor, leans against a thwart.

Oh look, a Wilson's Snipe.

A what?

Listen. You hear them first. The whirl-a-gig bird we called them.

He listens, hears a crooked propeller.

She's looking for a mate. That's the song and dance. Not a song really. It's the wind in her feathers.

I thought snipe were a joke.

They are, but they're real too. Listen. Beautiful. Oh the bird makes me happy.

It is something. A flute made of feathers.

Who would think they would survive this?

One bird anyway.

There must be another one somewhere. There couldn't be just one.

Maybe.

Maybe what?

Maybe there's only one.

The feathers sing the air again. Bird stops paddling so they can hear better. The canoe glides, then a series of little waves rock the canoe. Oil shimmers on the angles of wake. He watches the Woman's shoulders shivering. The snipe rises and falls, swoops and climbs over the pond.

How much longer can she keep flying I wonder.

Bird says nothing. Resumes paddling.

Land ho, says Bird. Welcome to the new world. She overcomes cramped legs and stands. Steps out onto the beach spread with pine cones and needles. Takes two steps and collapses on the sand.

Bird hauls the canoe into the trees, turns it over then comes back. He picks her up and walks toward the cabin. The back door in the woodshed is open. When they come inside something scuttles away in the wood pile.

The place is dry. Hasn't been ransacked. Hard to believe. Bottle flies blacken the window sills. Cobwebs. Specks of flyshit on everything. Bird puts the Woman on the couch, finds blankets in a chest. Tries to take her pulse at the wrist but he's never been good at that. Rope welts on the skin. Pools of purple under the eyes.

We can rest here.

He sinks into the recliner and ratchets back. The footrest rises and takes the weight off his legs. He can see the pond a sheet of black glass.

Probably had brook trout at one time.

Oh, maybe still. If there's a snipe.

Maybe.

Later, tremors wake them. The camp cracking like an old ship. His own tremors spilling on the earth.

The malady of oils. Spasdic endings of contaminated nerves. A glass wiggles to the edge of a shelf and falls off.

Hey, her voice is tremorous too. Tender in the night. Bird hears and says nothing. When reply is a burden.

Hey, her voice in the dark again, a soft pitch black no gleam of star. No reflection, no shadow in the inkiness. It could come to this, the whole goddamned thing blind. Hadn't we been blind all along, the masters of self deception.

I know you're awake.

No, she couldn't. No way he hadn't moved an inch, even held his breath.

Bird closes his eyes. Doesn't want to talk. His stomach aches and he wonders if it's more than hunger. One of those rapid response diagnoses, you've got a month to live, maybe less. But there's food here, something in cans. When it gets light open some cans.

A shadow at the stove. Blue orange flame under the pot and a dim hand stirring. Oatmeal. Grainy whiffs of hot cereal and her hair tied back and the flame on her neck. She walks across the room bowl in one hand candle in the other. Sets them on the table and goes back for the other bowl. Gathers the blankets around her in a kind of toga. He looks at her in the candlelight.

Why doesn't it get light.

He looks at the pond. No reflections. No one thing distinguishable from another.

You know why it doesn't get light. Hmm, I might have to keep you on as cook.

Don't be an asshole.

Sorry.

Seems natural for you.

So.

Just never mind. She sobs, drops her spoon.

Bird stands up and goes outside to get away. There are shapes of trees. The pond vague but still luminous. At the back of the cabin the cliffs rise in featureless shadow. He walks to the pond and edges a toe into the water. Takes off his clothes and drops them in the sand. The water rises to his ankles, then his calves, knees. His fish belly body sinks into the black water. He frogs away from the land, attempts to spread the oil slick away from his body. Reaches for the bottom with a toe, but the water is too deep.

His naked body is phosphorescent. The Woman stands in the window holding a candle. Treading water, he lifts a hand for her to see. She is the only person in the world who knows where he is, if he should go down. Where his bones would be. She stands still, maybe she can't see him anyway.

He knocks before going in. Thumbs the iron latch.

Just me, he says, stepping inside naked, dripping, his pants and shirts draped over his arm. The pictures of the dead man's family fall on the floor and he leans over and picks them up. She sits on the couch with her legs under blankets leaning a small book toward the candle. She'd lit the oven for him and he stands in front holding out his hands to warm.

It's not bad, you should try it.

No thanks. She doesn't look, turns a page and keeps reading. He hangs his clothes on some nails in the wall near the stove. Finds some clothes in a dresser, a pair of jeans, a plaid shirt with piping across the shoulders.

I thought you might want some heat. She puts the book down spine up on the table.

You can damage a book like that.

She picks up the book and closes it and puts it back on the table.

She twists her hair between two fingers.

What is your name?

She looks at him. Why did you come back to the hut?

I saw that animal in the woods. He was moving toward your place but I kept my business and went the other way. Changed my mind later.

We got off on the wrong foot.

Hmm.

I was scared.

Hmm.

I'm tired.

Take the bunk room, I'll stay out here.

How safe are we here?

Bird shrugs, You can end up on a spike no matter what.

I'd kill myself first.

You can say that, but...

Is this as light as it's going to get?

Thicker clouds. That's the trend.

To keep getting worse you mean, Darker all the time.

Yes.

When you're out in the pond treading water do you ever think of stopping.

Do you have anyone left?

Not that I know of.

I probably think about it every day. I thought about it tonight when I was out there.

And why not?

Bird stands up and walks over to the stove. I looked this way and saw you in the window.

I didn't know you could see me. She looks away.

I wonder how much gas is in those tanks.

You can turn it off it's plenty warm in here.

He pours water into a glass from the pitcher on the counter.

Did you piss in the pond when you were swimming?

Hmmm.

I guess I will lie down now.

There are clothes in those drawers when you get

up.

She stands and holds the blankets to her body as she walks to the back room. The springs stretch under her weight. After a minute he gets up and walks to the doorway.

I'm sorry about what happened.

He lies on the couch not sleeping. Her breath rattles in the back room. An owl hoots. No response. Maybe the last owl who knows. The wind scrapes a branch on the window.

Thunder rumbles. A low rolling ascension. He goes outside to pee and lightning lights up the hemlocks. He counts to seven before the thunder. Mile and a half. Far off lightning ignition of the oil soaked air. Flash and boom, flash and boom. Inside the Woman sits on the couch. They watch the foaming surface of the pond in the lightning strobes. Whitecaps. She hugs her arms to her chest. The interior of the cabin blinks like a strobe.

Quite the storm.

Umhmm, do you mind...

No.

You take the couch I'll lie here on the rug.

Don't do that.

Her hand rests on the sofa between them.

Bird pulls up his legs and stretches out into the back of the sofa. She slides into the middle puts her head down. Lifts her legs onto the couch. He puts an arm around her middle and pulls her in.

After a little while, breathing.

Kind of like the snipe isn't it.

What.

This, like snipe.

Like the last of them you mean.

* * * *

He wakes cramped but feels her warmth under the blanket. The storm is gone and now a routine gray day.

What's that sound?

What? says Bird.

Something out there. She stands and crosses to the door.

You better come here.

We don't want any cats.

There's no cat.

What then?

She is back inside pulling the door shut, rags in the crook of her arm. She walks toward him rocking her arm side to side.

Now what? he says sitting. Oh Jesus, a baby. What the hell are we going to do with a baby. How the hell did someone drop a baby here and leave. The mother, someone must be here somewhere. He gets up and goes outside and circles the camp. He kicks a barrel and it rolls down the hill and splashes into the pond. He goes back inside.

Goddam it. A kid to feed and drag around the country. What are you doing?

Changing him. You could do something to help.

Would you mind telling me how we're going to travel cross country with a baby.

Look, I didn't ask to have you in my life but here you are. And this child didn't ask for us either, but here he is. That's the way it is in this world. I found a couple of old sheets. You can cut them up for diapers.

Diapers?

You heard me. There's a pair of scissors.

She throws the sheets in his lap and drops the scissors on the table, the baby riding on her hip, cradled in her left arm. It looks so natural. He picks up the scissors and cuts out a square and hands it to her.

I'll have to double these up, maybe triple, so make a bunch.

He cuts and piles squares. The edges are thready, and the corners don't line up.

Here, you hold the child while I make something to eat.

She walks to the counter and looks at the row of containers on the shelf.

Ployes. How about ployes?

Anything, really.

You just add water.

Then put something sweet on them.

Sure, something sweet.

Bird looks at the child. He sleeps, the mouth suckling. The skin is red and blotchy.

He's kind of homely.

Kind of the way you are.

Huh. Well how old do you think he is.

I don't know. Four months. Five.
Left on a porch in the middle of a thunderstorm.

Someone thought we're his best chance is what.

She spatulas the ployes out of the frying pan. This is a nice Griswold, she says.

Or leaving him was their best chance.

I'd like to thank the owners of this place, you know.

What are you talking about?

Don't raise your voice so much. You'll wake him. I'm saying it's a good place with a good frying pan. You can see your face in a Griswold, it's so smooth.

I'm wondering should we give this guy a name.

She looks over. The child's hand wrapped around Bird's finger.

You've got a little grip don't you fella.

Your food is ready.

She brings her plate over and sits down next to him. If you want to wait until I'm done I'll hold him while you eat.

That's all right I can do both at the same time.

Bird walks to the counter and shifts the child to one arm, picks up his plate and returns to his place. He rolls a ploy up in his fingers and eats.

Not bad. No, I mean considering everything. Not bad.

He looks at her. She has green eyes. Like melted glacier.

I need to go outside. Talk to the child. That's what they need.

He doesn't understand anything.

He understands as much as you do. Talk to him. I'm going to the outhouse.

It seems she is gone a long time. His eyes are heavy, and he moves to the soft chair, setttles the child in the crook of his arm.

Bird wake up, she shakes his shoulder. Wake up, what's the matter with you? Look. A boat. They're coming toward us. A grudging dawn has spread over the land.

He snaps to, the music of the anthem band like cold water on the face. Squints at the window. The band stands on the far shore. The trumpet player's feet are in the water. The bass drum rests on the belly of a Fat Man in black camo. The rowboat crossing the pond leads a widening vee of wake.

Fucking a.

Let's go, she says, gathering things.

Go, where?

The ladder.

What ladder?

The ladder on the cliff.

The baby can go in here then on your back.

She holds a backpack. Bird looks out the window. The skiff and crew of camo men are in the middle of the pond.

The hemlocks conceal the first section of ladder, which follows a natural chimney in the rock face. At first they are hidden from below, but the first ladder stops at a ledge and the next section starts several feet to the right, ascends to another ledge. In a couple of minutes they are over the treetops and exposed. They can see the band on the shore across the pond but not the boat.

We have no idea where we're going, says Bird.

At the next ledge there is a bench. She coughs and sits down. Looks at her hand. Bird looks up the next ladder disappearing into the sky. He wishes there was a way to cut the ladders loose. He looks at the Woman.

Thank you for carrying the baby.

When they are a few feet up the third section the band stops playing. Pings on the rocks around them.

They're shooting.

The ladder curves away above them.

How much further?

Lead ricochets off the ladder above the Woman's

head. We're there.

She extends a hand. Touches the rim of the backpack.

He slept through that.

Let's keep moving off this ridge. We don't know who else is around here.

You're about to find out.

A large blue cavalry hat topping a head of yellow hair steps out from the cover of jack pines. When Bird makes a move toward the little man three more men emerge from the trees and stand behind him. Bird stops, moves closer to the Woman and child.

The short blonde man looks the Woman up and down and smiles.

Well boys got ourselves a sports car. Indeed. You like to ride do you sweetheart. Now put the backpack on the ground and step away from it.

Who the hell are you?

A staff sweeps the air and belts Bird in the ribs.

He doubles over, sinks to the ground. The child starts to whimper. When the Woman bends over to pick him up a staff trips her and she rolls to the ground.

What the hell is this, says the blond cavalryman. A little family?

The sounds of the anthem band roll up over the cliff again.

She picks up a rock and throws it at the blond man. He dodges, but his hat falls to the ground. The thick yellow hair fringes a bald pate. She thinks he has a small head and that it is misshapen somehow. He must wear the hat to hide the deformity. The little man reddens, picks up his blue hat and settles it back on his head with both hands. The three camo men shift on their feet.

Excuse me, Blue Hat rants. What I doing here standing top this fucking cliff talking to myself? Is this the summit my respect? No pun intended. Right men? You know I'm talking about, don't you men?

Yes sir.

Yes sir.

Yessir sir.

Yes sir. See, these men their duty. But you little kitten someone got you first. Captain jealous. Huh, you hard hearing or what. He walks to her side and kicks her in the back of the knees.

Bird finds himself thinking a deficit man will be deficit in language.

Hands, says Blue Hat, pick up that child and give it me.

No one moves. The three camo men shuffle and twitch. One on one Bird'd kill this son of a bitch with his bare hands. Crush the scrawny neck. The three men in black are another story.

Hands, when I say something you jump.

Yes sir.

I said pick that screaming thing and bring it me.

Yes sir.

Have you ever felt the paling your asshole Hands.

No sir.

There's a first time for everything Hands.

Yes sir.

Hands before you pick that child and bring it me I want you kick that man and Woman. Do you understand me Hands.

I think so sir.

You think so. The little blond man's mouth curves into a tight smile.

He smiles at Stephen.

Soldier Stephen knock Hands to the ground by reason of stupidity. Discipline is key men. And obedience. Without discipline and obedience there is nothing. Understood?

Yes sir.

That screaming is driving me crazy. Pick up that child and bring here Stephen.

Yes sir. Stephen picks up the child, bounces him a little bit.

He is pretty cute Captain. Take a look. Hey little guy, it's ok. It's going be all right now.

The blond man takes the child in his hands and holds him at arm's length. The child fusses, and the blond man frowns.

The future is not the place for you young man, sad to say. No. What we have in common. The land is red. The storm in our souls has wrought this ruin. We have striven against ourselves. Conspired against the likes of youth, sad to say, and this with my own heart sewn with mere thin thread. So there then, people, this is the fate of innocence.

Hah! Gaddup! Hup! Hup!

He runs toward the edge of the cliff. He pulls up short but the child flies over the edge. Twelve eyes follow the fluttering white blankets sail out over the rimrock and fall out of sight. A vortex of silence. The oiled sky meets the crown of hemlock forest. A mile away across the pond the horns in the anthem band flutter the air. The blond man stands on the rim, his right hand holding on to the brim of his large blue hat.

The Woman wraps her arms around her head.

Ahhhh.

Soldier Stephen drops to his knees. Hands'
mouth hangs. The blond man composes himself and
strides back into the middle of the group.

So there we are men. So there men. You see the
efficacy, I am sure. My reality will carry this forsaken
world no doubt. Call the trucks, Hands. We will see
these two sorry souls back to the Stadium to await their
own reality. Fine men. Mission accomplished.

*****

Bird joins the line of men standing with their
fingers crooked into the weave of hurricane fence. All
day their eyes follow the paling trucks coming and going.
When a truck leaves the camo men mock the prisoners,
holding a stick and doing knee bends.

One morning the big doors are swinging shut and
jam with a steely screech. A commotion erupts outside.

Several camo men run toward the opening to see what's going on but pull up short and scramble back inside just as a raging mammoth explodes through the opening. His right rear leg drags a man tangled in a rope. The man tries to grab the rope wound around his ankle but the mammoth moves too fast. The man reaches, falls back, reaches, falls back. His head bounces in the dirt.

The creature swarms into the middle of the Stadium field then pulls up. His entrapment dawning, he swings his massive legs forward and back, side to side. The tethered man no longer has the strength to pick himself up. A crew of handlers run in carrying leg irons and chain. Chain so heavy it bends the men down. They struggle with the restive beast. He swings a leg and catches a man in the knees. The man folds in half, his head collapsing toward his feet. Shattered femurs stick out through his pants.

Another man runs toward the downed man. He bends to grab the downed man arms when the mammoth's leg comes back again. The rescuer's severed head rolls away in the dust. A cheer rises along the hurricane fence.

This here's some good entertainment.

Of all the channels there is and we get this one.

Our own reality show.

There is no reality anymore.

The two men left standing retreat. There's confusion who's in charge. More men run in. Blue Cavalry Hat appears on the field.

Blue Hat, Blue Hat's here, whispering up and down the fence. Men sitting on the ground behind the standing prisoners get up and come forward to see what's happening. The little man strides into the fray uncoiling a whip.

Most ruthless son of a bitch walked the earth.

Not a man wouldn't kill his ass with a chance.

Even his own men thinks that way.

What happens screw around with mother nature.

A product of genie modification they say.

Genetic engineering stupid. And it's true. Why his head is weird that way.

You mean like the same as corn got that way and

wheat so you couldn't eat em they did to his brain?

Moot anyway.

He is an advanced and efficient human being.

The personality of frozen clay.

If even.

But modified.

Look at this.

Blue Hat twirls the whip about in a circle his right hand high over his head.

Think he's a fucking cowboy or what.

Taciturn like one.

What?

Yeah but that ain't no bull.

He'll figure that out.

Blue Hat moves to his right toward the rear of

the animal, the whip spinning over his head.

Like he's casting.

Just another Izaak Walton.

Who?

Jesus he is.

The slender tail of the whip shoots toward the folded man. He has just propped himself on an elbow, rolled the bloody head away. Then the whip loops his neck and Blue Hat drags him clear of the mammoth. The broken legged man chokes. Hands go to his throat trying to pull the whip off.

Jesus H. Christ.

Thought I seed everything but I guess not.

Well he saved him, I guess. Maybe he did, maybe didn't.

Got a chance now didn't before.

Discipline gentlemen. That's what we're about here. Defending our freedom and way of life. Whatever the threat.

Psychopath.

Bred and borned here in the old USA.

Father was a generalissimo the old military I hurd.

Runs in the family.

Blue Hat drags the man twenty feet. Walks in and uncoils the whip from the man's neck.

There's section on that string got razor knives set in.

Man's psycho like I said.

He hears that your head will roll.

Listen I don't give a shit.

There now men, shouts Blue Hat, coiling his whip into precise loops. We can't have stupidity around here, just can't. What would come of us being stupid like this fellow here. Got his legs broke back. And now what we do with him? Are we going to spend resources saving stupidity. I think not. Let's remove these souls and start over, shall we? Secure legs of beast without further ado.

Further ado?

Look, here come the suits.

Uh oh. That's never good.

Checking up Blue Hat.

He's grew a moustache.

Always had one.

Had not.

Look more suits up top.

Don't point at'em.

No.

Don't look neither.

No.

The Presidents of Impaling.

Fuckers.

They still ain't got a single leg.

Blue Hat's going take charge. Watch this.

Bird stands apart from the men hanging along the fence with their fingers hooked in the mesh.

You. You know where they keep the women?

Good luck with that Bud. You got a woman in here?

Maybe.

Like I said.

Shouts swell from the field. Two men struggle with a leg hold at the end of the chain. Blue Hat watches, fingering the coils of his whip. Half a dozen suits who had moved in close to look at the mammoth realize the danger and back away.

I thought we were done stupid, Blue Hat screams. That was my lesson a short time ago. It's like short memory disease epidemic around here.

The whip flies from Blue Hat's right hand toward the two handlers working at the rear of the mammoth. They hear the crease of air and duck. The slender snake recoils, as if gauging distance, then returns at terrific speed and slices off the left ear of the near man. He claps a hand to the side of his head. Stares at his ear lying in the dust.

Holy shit.

Yeah.

How'd he do that.

That was luck.

Hold there, screams Blue Hat to the second man who had turned and started to run the other way.

Uh oh.

Yeah.

I'd keep running.

Where to?

The second man stops, turns, starts, clouds with indecision. The black coil sweeps in low and cracks off below his belt shredding his pants. Blood soaks down both pant legs. The man claps his hands to his crotch and collapses without a sound.

Castration.

He meant that.

Yeah.

Man's psycho.

Even the suits turn their heads. One covers his eyes.

Now men. Is there any more stupid here? Might as well get it over with. His white teeth fierce behind the thin and trim mustache.

Those suits is even scared of him.

Look they got that leg finally.

Steak for supper.

Not for us.

At one end of the field workers prepare a fire under a long metal grill. A man sharpens knives on a stone slab. Up in the sky boxes the suits and high heels sip drinks, laugh, survey the spread of Stadium. The bands are in full swing, and ragged synchronicity. Four march clockwise, and four march counterclockwise around the ramparts. The flames of a hundred torches flicker the perimeter. In the shadows the black camo lookouts strut round and round.

Count the souls on your right divide by twenty. That's how many days you got left. They work from right to left always. Inventory is dropping though for some reason. They've not brought anyone since you got here.

You know much about this place?

Ain't much to know really.

Where do they keep the women?

Women. Ha. Better not waste your time my friend. Women. On the other side back in the corridors, all levels. They ain't that many anyway, but Blue Hat ranks 'em when they come in One to Five. The One's go up there with the suits and working down the Fives right across the way here.

Christ.

The barbarian brain is a ballbuster you might say. You sayin you got someone among them women.

Not really.

Well that's good then. More peace of mind to ya on that account.

Peace of mind?

Ya.

Bird watches the mammoth. Since the handlers' secured one rear leg the spectators turn brazen again. A few suits with women and drinks stroll in close. Someone in a group at the rear of the animal points up at the genitals and laughs. During his encounter in the meadow Bird had seen the beer keg size testicles and five foot dongs.

They say the cum fills a five gallon pail, says the Bearded Man.

That's a lot to swallow.

Not for the girl critters it ain't. Everythins in proportional.

The miracle of science, huh. Ain't it a wonder.

Hey buddy. A small man jostles Bird's elbow. Bird moves away. The man steps close again and bends his head toward Bird.

Hey, ah, you the one carried the baby up the ladder, huh. The man steps back watches Bird over his shoulder.

How'd you know?

Oh. The little man steps away again. The furtive eyes don't land anywhere for long. I know some things.

Renewed yelling from the field rises over the din of the bands. Prisoners who had drifted away school back to the fence like fish, hitch their fingers in the warp of wire. The mammoth has freed one leg and is using the leverage to loosen the other chains. He tears the right rear anchor out of the ground then rears back and pulls out the two front stakes. A cheer rises from the men on the fence.

The handlers run back into the arena. The Blue Hat follows, uncoils his black snake.

What the hell's he going to do now?

As if a shoelace would tame a mammoth.

This should be good.

They shoulda hat the legs shackled each other.

Huh.

Blue Hat loops the whip out slow, speeds up, then sends the snake flying. The honed blades slice into the mammoth's leg above the knee. The flesh opens and spills out a crooked rill of blood that runs down the leg, spreads a delta across the foot.

That's jus goine piss the big fella off.

Hat's shit for brains.

I wouldn't say that loud.

Forward back, forward back. The whip master Blue Hat dances on the balls of his feet.

Spryly.

Quick son of a bitch.

Said he was a prizefighter. Killed a couple of guys with his fists.

That little shit?

Seems there's always someone used to be a prize fighter somewhere.

Don't doubt it. Just like there's a fat lady.

The barbed tongue slashes the creature's left ear. A foot long flap drops and dangles by strings of flesh.

This ain't goin end good.

Not for man nor beast.

The prisoners jostle and blabber at Bird's back. Some try to move close to the fence for a better view. Others want to get away. The smell of them. He lifts his head for air. The little Bearded Man reappears at his side stroking himself with his right hand. Bird shoves him away.

It's the blood does it. Blood over babe for me any day.

You're a pathetic little man.

Yes I am. But we're all going to die.

Bird clenches the fence. He feels like snapping the little man's neck.

Blue Hat drives his snake through the air. Suits, camo men, the prisoners, all eyes watch. The anthem bands don't skip a beat. A handful of women mingle in the crowd of suits. Bird scans the top tier of boxes for her. It hadn't occurred to him until now. Of course she would be at the top.

The action on the field unfolds. For some reason the doors at the south end of the stadium swing open and freedom gleams through the opening. The creature rears up, sweeps the air with his front legs, chains clanking, the leg irons tracing deadly arcs. Even Blue Hat recoils before the giantism of the creature. The handlers still on the field retreat and press against the walls.

The doors have opened for two paling trucks

returning from a day's work on the Avenue. Blue Cavalry Hat skillfully works the whip into a long graceful esse curve, winds up backstroke, and then leaves the ground hurling the pitch of the whip in a flat singing arc toward the beast. The spikes rip the right eye from its socket and the huge orb dangles from bloody strands.

The men at the fence step back. Three stories up the suits recoil from the plate glass. The one eyed mammoth takes off toward the open doors. The truck drivers who at first stepped out of their vehicles now scramble back into the trucks. The prisoners cheer, and crowd the fence. Heads appear again in the upper windows. The mammoth runs with his head sideways trying to compensate for his loss of bilateral vision. Chains and stakes fly. Blue Cavalry Hat jogs after him coiling the bloodied whip with his left hand.

Confused by the trucks between him and the doors the mammoth veers right, scatters a group of handlers attempting to approach along the Stadium wall. A cry rises from the prisoners. The mammoth swings left and smashes into the lead paling truck, rolling it onto its side, and then it disappears out the doors, bellowing in pain and rage.

Blue Cavalry Hat stands alone in the middle of the arena. The coiled whip hangs off his shoulder.

The injured start to pick themselves up, if they can, and assess wounds. The men in the pens slink back from the wire once more. The bands' volume turns down, and people look up to see what is the matter. A breeze bends the flames at the top of the ramparts.

Told nothing good come of it.

Man's a psychopath.

Shhhh.

That's what I call cruelty to animals.

Never mind the people.

Never's been this quiet here.

Forgotten such a thing.

Blue Cavalry Hat scans the ramparts questioning the silence. Someone blows a trumpet note. After a pause another horn bleats a few plaintive notes of taps. One by one horns fall in, the trumpets, trombones, saxophones, and flugelhorns. It only stopped for a minute. The sound track is back.

A flawed fanfare for the common man.

A bass drum booms, and other drums follow. The patriotic anthem restores the band cacophony.

Told nothing good come of it.

Critter's out of here.

The soundtrack is back.

Coulda had a steak.

Not us.

Wonder what become of the little fella.

It ain't right, whipped like that.

Not after we mixed up the DNA and bringed him back and everything.

We made them 'stinct in the first place.

Only one theory.

Oh yeah what's yours?

Aliens stopping here looking for food.

Dinosaurs beat them out I hurd.

Science says it was volcano dust blocked the sun and made things too cold for 'em.

And that was before all this climate crap we got now, right?

Yep.

Look here. The show must go on.

Business as usual.

A new pair of paling trucks enter the arena grounds from the maintenance garages. They are already loaded with the day's inventory of prisoners. Another load of heads bobbling over the top of the wood slatted sides. The trucks swing into the slant of daylight falling through the big doors, pass the crews cleaning up after the debacle caused by Blue Cavalry Hat.

Another load.

Another day older and deeper in debt.

St Peter don't you call me cause I can't go.

I owe my soul to the company store.

Fee fye fo fum, doodledee dum.

Bird slouches into a wall at the end of the hurricane fence, and tries to ignore the smell and jibberish of the crowd. Scans the upper tiers of the Stadium looking for the Woman. Men on the field start cleaning up the mess at the big doors. They attach chains to the tipped over truck, and pull it back onto its tires. They wrap two corpses in black plastic, wind them with loops of duct tape at the head, ankles, and middle, and lay them in the back of a battered F-150.

The small Bearded Man materializes at his elbow again.

What?

With time short like this don't want to miss an opportunity, eh? He moves closer though he faces away talks backwards over his shoulder and pumps himself with his right hand.

Little excitement takes your mind off things, eh? Nothing like a little blood to keep the loins exercised, eh? He finishes and buttons up his pants. Bird steps away but the Bearded Man steps in closer. Licks his fingers and combs them through his white beard. What is it with old men and their typical white beards thinks Bird.

Eh, my friend. A message from Hands. His forefinger hangs on his bottom teeth His eyes twist their focus on Bird.

Hands?

Whose baby that was carried up the ladder wants to thank you the Woman.

The Bearded Man puts his hand back inside his shirt.

What?

Yes, wants thank you the lady.

Who does, what are you talking about?

Don't matter that. The Bearded Man employs himself for a minute, edges away, sidles back backwards, looking over his shoulder, his eyes spinning in their sockets.

Only I ever wanted was someone let me love them, see. But I was too strange. Never happens and now this. He waves his arm at the throng of men at the fence. Big ass fuck now. They say some guys get off and go out with the biggest hardon ever. Ain't that sumthin. Four, five days, my count.

What's this about Hands?

Oh that. Well, see for favors I get information. I might be crazy, but I'm not you know, really crazy. No, I'm not. They wants to thank you, and they hates The Blue Cavalry Hat most of all. Then Bearded Man goes silent, turns around in a circle. Just checking the perimeter, if you know what I mean.

Ah.

It's a long story, isn't it, before Adam and Eve even. Before monkeys. When do you think the first fuck was? You know what I mean? The real thing. None of this cell splitting stuff. I mean do we even know what came first the fucking or the egg? Huh? Do we know anything?

We had our chances.

Look friend I don't know where you go from here other than the poles, but be ready. You have an ally will help you out is why. Just watch out for stupid like the ringmaster says. We don't have time for stupid. The Bearded Man puts his fingers back in his mouth, rolls his eyes, and melts into the crowd.

Rumors swirl through the Stadium. From prisoners to camo men to suits. Speculation there will be public punishment. Possible example Blue Cavalry Hat. More rumors dispel the idea of authority being questioned publicly.

The next morning when the big doors open and the trucks pull in to load up the mood in the pens is somber. Black camo men count twenty five men from the south end, and march them into the personnel truck. The prisoners by turns watch, turn their heads away as two rows of bobble heads in the back of the truck move away.

Just then one of the prisoners leaps from the bench onto the top of the truck cab and starts ranting.

See here human rights are the eaten apple, the rotten core it's a pister mister oh yeah we're agoin to the rodeo eo eo play it again Sam fuck the Stadiums kill the crooked suits crooked corrupt cretinous creatures that's the spindrift mister a pisser lying bunch of cheap shit bastards.

Spittle flies in his words. Two men try to pull him back into the truck but they pull down his pants instead. Naked from the waist now he steadies himself on the roof of the cab and pisses on the truck's windshield .

The truck driver hits the brakes, the tires skid in the dust. The ranter falls spread eagled onto the hood of the truck, rolls down over the grill and hits the ground. The wheels miss him but while the man raises himself on one knee, the second truck changes course and speeds up. The impact is a plock a soft hollowness. The trucks continue out the doors, leaving the broken body in the dust. Some of the pen men turn away, others rake the fence with sticks and rocks and scream at the trucks. The big doors swing shut.

Blue Cavalry Hat walks over and stands next to the body. Whip wire coiled in his left hand

That's all she wrote.

What was that about.

Last word in edgewise I guess.

Nothin goin stop'em.

Blue Cavy Hat in control.

How's that son of a bitch always right there.

Here he goes.

Now men. Now. Anyone want to add to that?

His eyes scan the fence. Eyes turn down, aside. Blue Cavalry Hat kicks the corpse.

Don't look a wild animal in the eyes.

See men, this Stadium is a venue for free speech, always has been. Ever man can say what he wants any time. Like this fellow here had his say. Anyone can have their say. Nothing stopping. You see now the satisfaction comes with speaking your mind.

Blue Cavy Hat walks a lap around the dead man, and then kicks him in the back with his steel toed black leather boots.

So men, any takers. The soapbox is all yours. We stand by free speech here always have. So who's next? Someone must have something to say, hmmm? A comment on the fine music, perhaps, the accommodations? He looks up and down the length of the pens. Then he steps away from the dead man, skips, and kicks him in the face.

Jesus H.

Fuckin A.

Shhh.

What would happen if we all rushed him?

Kick 'em dead.

Dance on his head.

Spill his blood red.

Blue Cavalry Hat drops a couple of whip coils and flicks the black line into the air. Like launching a kite. More loops drop off his fingers, and the line hisses. The little man kicks his heels and dances calligraphy, his spindly legs tracing eulogy for the fallen man. He belts out some memory of olden aria.

One kind of theater.

Man, leather, and song one thing.

Man can dance.

Crazy is all one thing of it.

Dance of the dead. Dance on his head.

Never seen...

I can't watch anymore.

Seen this movie before.

Uh, now what's that, no, earthquake.

Fuck me, we're going to die here.

Not again.

His dance done it.

Demon dance of the earth.

The ground wobbles and the men sway, grab the
wire. Some drop to their knees. The floor cracks, shifts,
heaves. All fours. Knocked down. Concrete shards pell
mell down from the ramparts. Dust and stone spit

from the walls. A minute, two. Rattle and roll. Wait it, wait it out. Cover your head with your arms. After two minutes, three minutes, forever when the earth is falling apart. Eyes turn to the middle of the field where Blue Cavalry Hat lies sprawled over the dead man. His whip punctuating the pink soil.

Little man lost his hardon.

This place is a tomb.

Wowser. Warn't built for earthquakes like we got now.

Nothin was.

Still ain't up.

The demise of the main attraction.

We can't lose our entertainment channel.

No but look at this.

The man run over by the truck and left for dead struggles out from under Blue Cavalry Hat and raises himself up on one knee.

That is one tough SOB.

Still, same old story, where do you go?

Borrowed time.

A prolongation at best.

A what?

The shaking starts again, slow like the vibration from a truck passing. It drags on, and the men look at each other. A violent spasm wrenches the ground and knocks people to the ground. Men cradle their heads in their arms. Fumaroles of concrete dust spume out of the structure. The anthem bands falter.

I say, this place is a tomb.

Bird lays on the floor next to the fence. It's impossible to stand. Men crawl. A scream of steel, a sound shock tears the ears. A section of the sliding roof long unused twists out of it's track and crashes down into the field. Tons of steel suspended by braided cables sways back and forth like a pendulum. Lightning flashes an orange luminescence in the sky.

It's not nice to mess with mother nature.

Too late.

Mother's been raped.

We's raped ourselves.

I promise to be nice from now on.

I'll start recycling.

No more whiskey for me I promise.

The crowd moans, the ground shakes, and the concrete cracks. Gray dust charges the oiled air. Men tear their shirts and hold the cloth over their faces. The lights blinker, go dark, blinker, go dark. The rampart fires cast orange shadow on the faltering bands, figures shape-shift in the pale lightning.

Well my friend the gods are smiling, no? The Bearded Man lies on the ground next to Bird. He faces away, twists his head to talk back over his shoulder. His eyes are buggy.

Like I said, Hands is a helping hand.

What?

It's a hard day's night I know.

Another tremor rumbles through the arena.

Whoa Nelly. Hang on.

Like I said, it's over when it's over. But look here. It's your time.

Next to Bird's head a pair of shears cuts the wire fence. Snap. Snap. On the other side a black watch cap low on the forehead comes close.

I told you, says the Bearded Man.

Hold onto this rope. Lose me and you're lost.

I can die here, muses Bird, or I can die somewhere else. I might as well follow the rope.

Now skinny out of there. The voice under the watch cap.

I didn't come here alone and I'm not leaving alone.

I know about that.

Bird turns the rope around his wrist. The tremors taper off. He shinnies under the wire and stands up on the other side. The dark man's shoulders rise over Bird's head.

Don't get lost, says the man. Let's go and hold the hell on. Now listen, from here up we go three sets of stairs. Then we're gonna pay a visit to your girlfriend's suite.

She's not my girlfriend.

S'no time for definitions.

He strides out, half drags Bird faltering on stiff legs, enters a closed stairwell. The big man counts out, One, two, three, four, five, six, seven, eight, nine, landing turn, one, two, three, four, five, six, seven, eight, nine landing turn...

Coming down, says a voice from above. Bird freezes but the dark man jerks him forward.

Coming up, right of way, he yells.

On the outside, says the voice above.

Inside track here, the dark man in the dark.

Who are you?

Electricians.

I hope you get this place up and running soon.

Oh yeah.

They emerge on a balcony high over the field with an open railing on the one side and a row of doors on the other. Dark Man stops in front of an unmarked door and knocks.

Electricians, he yells.

A thin man with blue blood and a thin mustache wearing a red silk robe tied with gold sash opens the door. He smokes a thin black cigarette through a thin glass holder. A perfect part bisects his oiled hair and his lips are lipsticked ruby red.

Gentlemen, he purses, something tells me you are not electricians.

A draft gutters the candles in the jade wall sconces. Animal skins cover the floor. A lion, two brown bears, a white bear, something else catlike. A wall of leather bound books. Red stains on an embroidered white table cloth, and broken crystal on the floor. He holds an open bottle of Chateau Lafite 1869 in his left hand.

I have just lost my best wine to the earthquake or I would offer you a glass.

I'm fine with a PBR if you got that, says the dark man.

Excuse me?

The thin man looks at the men's shoes. The thin snobs always go for your shoes thinks Bird.

But I can offer you a glass of Mouton de la St Aubriessenete 1943. A thin smile spreads the thin man's thin lips.

Thank you, says the Dark Man.

It's nice you can appreciate something fine, says the thin man, still smiling.

I think so. Dark Man picks up the full bottle of Mouton de la Aubriessenete, lifts it to his lips and tips it straight up. The liquid glugs through the neck and sloshes down his throat. When the bottle is empty he throws it against the window.

The three men stand on the back of the polar bear. Beyond the window, obdurate chaos.

I suppose when the common man shows appreciation for something fine it's not a bad thing. Now, gentlemen...

Well..., says dark man.

Elizabeth, please.

Her hands reach through the curtains and pull them open. The Woman steps through and stands still. She wears a low red shirt and tight red sweater in the way of Stadium women. A necklace of turquoise medallions fans across her chest. She shows no recognition of Bird.

The dark man whistles. The thin man closes his eyes.

Bird looks at the thin man. He guesses the thin man and the Woman have saved each other somehow. She is his disguise.

Time here is not long, says thin man. He hands

the Woman a jacket.

There are three flights down, says the dark man, a quarter mile of tunnel then you're on your own.

Outside, lightning flick flacks the sky. The music congeals, the bands in disarray. Instruments have been damaged. Men throw more wood on the fires. The fires must never go out.

Out of nowhere the dark man steps up and slaps the Woman on the mouth, then the thin man. Both drip blood from the lower lip.

What the hell?

The blow collapses the Woman against Bird's knees, but she stands up and swift kicks the dark man between the legs.

Apparently asshole your mother never taught you manners.

Never had no mother. He bends over holding his crotch with both hands.

I think we should go now, says Bird.

The Woman and Bird move well but the dark man is slow. He coughs, and becomes winded. They are almost blind in the tunnel, but now and then a bare bulb blinks. At one lamp black moths flutter at the light.

The electricity's back.

Maybe.

Does it matter?

A bare incandescent bulb wavers under the arch of wet, mossy concrete. They watch electrons pulsing on the wire. Cobwebs draped. Counting the intervals, one bulb darkness, two bulb darkness, three bulb. Dark Man bends at the waist, throws up, falls down, hands clutching his chest, blood and black moths. He flops onto his back, eyes roll into the back of his head.

Shit, she kneels beside him. Fingers look for a pulse.

Cardiac arrest, she says, watching the man's face. She bends over him, pinches his nose with her left hand.

You sure about this? says Bird.

No, compressions isn't it? She moves over the big man's chest, clamps her left hand on top of her right and pushes down.

You kick this guy in the balls and now you're trying to save him? Let's just get on with it.

The Woman pumps twenty times and then tilts the head back and leans in to breathe.

I don't remember the sequence, do you?

When she leans in the man convulses and ejects a stream of vomit into her point blank face. She falls back, the acid burning her eyes and nose. She throws up into her hands, and looks queerly into the moths' fluttering the bulb's umbra. Water leaking out of the ceiling drips. Bird turns away with dry heaves. She wipes her mouth with the dark man's shirt.

Jesus, says Bird, I'm not sure the sequence matters.

She cleans Dark Man's mouth with the tail of his shirt. A moment later he sputters and opens his eyes.

You're alive, you can get up now. We have to keep moving.

His eyes open and the void fills in.

The light bulb blinks out. Comes on. Goes out. Blackness again, nothingness.

Fuck.

Where to?

This way.

This way?

Sounds of the man getting on his feet.

Up ahead another light bulb blinking. A blizzard of white moths this time. A thousand wings flap fly into their hair, eyes, wing dust tints the air.

Keep your mouths shut. The Woman sinks to her knees and throws up again.

Need air.

Need air.

They emerge from the tunnel into a forest of scrub oak and a smudgy realm of gray air. The hulky shadow of the Stadium looms a quarter mile away.

*****

Well, well. Here we are once again. Seems you folks are fond of travel. Peace is the absence of nationalism my friends. Freedom can only be achieved sans state. We smother ourselves in self congratulatory, self aggrandizing, self revelatory selfishness. Paens to anthropomorphic arrogance, and we have filled the oceans with burning water.

Hat taps his whip against his thigh. The Bearded Man stands at his shoulder.

Told ya, told ya.

Shut up whiskers. The Dark Man, huh? I'm surprised. I had you a species of intellect.

You had nothin you yellow piece of shit.

The Bearded Man whoops around Blue Cavalry

Hat like a wounded bird while Hat's right arm lifts into a circle and arcs the razor snake toward Dark Man's neck. His arm takes the strike that draws blood, but the whip is in his grasp and he jerks Blue Hat off balance. Bearded Man looks surprised, but then jumps onto Blue Hat's back and stabs him in the neck.

I been wanting this.

He bears down on the handle and twists. A technique he remembers seeing in a movie. Blue Cavalry Hat collapses to the ground.

Finally, sings Bearded Man. I done something worthwhile.

Bearded Man gets up. Pulls his knife out of the neck and looks at the blade before wiping it off on the dead man's shirt. Kicks Blue Cavalry Hat in the head.

Eh, little shit of a man. Kicks Blue in the head again. How you like that medicine huh? Picks up the blue hat and puts it on. Why they make men like this, huh? Somebody tell me why they make men like this.

He walks away several feet. Turns, runs at the body again. This one for my brother. Kicks. This one for my son. Kicks. Oh, he's dead, and I'm dead too, I'm dead too. Beard holds the point of his knife to his chest and falls forward to the ground.

* * * *

The three survivors move away from the Stadium following an old black top road. Small birch and aspens grow out of the crooked cracks. Leaves, moss, blackberry vines hide the blacktop. Sometimes the painted white stripes in the middle of the road appear. After a while there is no more sign of a road. The Dark Man's lungs are failing and the Woman and Bird slow for him to keep up.

Will they follow us? asks the Woman.

With Blue Hat gone no.

Seems like there's always someone to replace that sort of man. There's no getting rid of them.

There is more to worry about than a handful of people escaping. The place is falling apart.

Still.

He isn't with us.

Let him go.

Let's wait a minute. I don't mind a rest.

That was something. Bringing him back like that in the tunnel.

Didn't really think about it. Surprised me too. A shower would be nice.

I can think of a few things that would be nice.

Toothpaste and toothbrush.

A glass of clean water.

Clean clothes.

A salad.

Lemonade.

A dry chardonnay, chilled.

You're spoiled now.

I hope he didn't have another heart attack. We're out of there because of him. What's in it for him anyway.

A strange affiliation.

Look, Bird.

Huh?

Here we are,
In this mottle mull
Of ungreen forest.
Why us?

There's an island in the north.

So?

An island. That's it.

So?

It's beyond the reach of most things.

Am I going with you?

I don't know, are you?

Are you asking me?

Not really.

I'm going back to look.

Bird lies down under a hemlock tree and closes his eyes. The ground trembles. Large tree roots have cracked out of the ground, rent the soil. The sky boils with orange tinge. He wonders if there is time left for improvement. He wonders how long.

After dozing he gets up and one more time starts to follow her. He moves over the shambled forest, a soft sough of duff under foot, the ground that never dries out. Is there anything left to trust? He listens for diesel engines, the mammoths, the maniacal shouting, the delirious horns, the dumb drums, the population drunk on delusion. He wonders stupidly why he is going back to look for her again.

Sounds in the woods. Motion in the foliage. White shoulders, tangled hair. The Dark Man on his back under the roof of an old trail shelter. She straddles the seven feet of him. He wheezes. Coughs blood. His hands supporting her floating over him, lifting, dropping, lifting, dropping, ah the bitch, bitch. But. Who said otherwise?

She screams and he drops her, she screams and he drops her, she screams and he drops her, and she rolls off and lies on the ground. The seven foot man stands up and spits blood and clutches his chest, staggers and spits, pitches forward, sprawls full length on the ground dead as the proverbial doornail.

Check with your doctor to see if you are healthy enough for sex.

Bird watches the Woman sit up, extend her legs beyond the edge of the shelter and cross them. Reach for her pants, his pants, sitting for society tea, why, yes please I would, and I do thank you. Picks up her clothes, dresses, loses herself in the dirty, ill fitting clothes, stands and steps over the body, this time doesn't check a pulse. Hesitates. Stoops and turns the dead man's pockets inside out.

Bird leaves the way he came.

He hikes considering the beastiality of their abandon. Is that why she saved him, he wonders, porcelain and coffee, tastes his vomit so she can feel that cock inside her even at this stage of the game. The human game almost over and procreation moot. Not primal sex though, what takes the prize every time, seriously, primal sex.

Hikes for an hour, doesn't feel bad, doesn't feel good either. A landscape of blasted roots, burned branches, lightning flick flacky sky. Still, here and there an occasional green fuse.

* * * *

Now what's this? Sweet campfire smoke curling upward into the canopy of ancient hemlocks, and the smell of roasting meat, deer carcass on a spit, strips of brown meat hanging. The head of a doe lying on gnarled roots. Three severed legs. He picks a bloody knife up off a rock and leans over the fire and saws off a crooked piece. Hard to remember anything tasting so good.

That the manners you was raised with mister?

Bird spins around and drops the meat into the fire.

Goddamn and he's careless too.

The boy runs in and snatches the dropped meat from the ashes. Bird steps back. The kid might be fourteen, fifteen. He's thin and when he stands up he coughs the blood.

You alone?

What's it to you?

How'd you get the deer?

Snare.

Where'd you come from?

How do I know.

Anyone else out here with you.

No.

The kid licks his fingers. Leaps into a hemlock, clambers hand over hand into the canopy and disappears. Bird circles the tree, may be an eagle's nest up there. Carves more meat, stirs the fire with a stick, collects more wood, makes a place to lie down near the heat.

What do I have left? I might lie down and not

get up. I might. I might not. Maybe if I start counting and fall asleep the kid will come down the tree and hit me on the head and put me on the fire.

He wakes in the dark. Something different, blankets? An arm across his middle. Blankets. Breath on the back of his neck, a pulse of breath. Bad breath, and thin bones stretched along Bird's backside. The boy's sleeping fingers scuttle Bird's back. He stutters and coughs and Bird feels the spray on the back of his neck.

The spastic earth shakes them awake. Wet needles patter down from the hemlocks and hiss in the red embers. The deer meat is a misshapen black mass. The tremors shiver their bones.

Look at this sabotage of flesh, a wonder the boy puts an arm around me, but it's not like there's anyone else, is there?

On the other side of the fire the Woman stands watching them through the smoke. The Woman wearing buckskins. Never thought I would see her again. Her face in the smoke. And he still has his bones inside his skin.

Your guard is down.

Uh.

Deerslayer.

Not me. Moves the boy's arm aside and stands up. Him.

The Woman looks at the boy, back to Bird.

Hmmmm.

Hungry?

Me?

He cuts a charred chunk and passes it to her.

What happened?

He's dead.

Oh.

Couldn't save him this time.

Oh.

She chews abstractly.

Look. Company.

Shit. Now what?

Two men, dirty and disheveled the way men are. One extra, extra large and fat the way men are. One small and thin the way men are. Two men on the trail. Long hair, dark whiskered, dirty men.

They don't see the man and Woman by the fire. The man and Woman are invisible to them.

What's this a, a,   a,   fuckin pi..picnic?

I don't see no ants Daddy. Can't be a picnic if there ain't no ants.

Shaddup you bloody eejet.

No devilish eggs neither. No picnic basket, no bottle wine and glass. No cheese or tapenade, no rarebit or rabbit, or folded napkins neither. No picnic. Just a black carcass of a dead something. Maybe related to that dead deer head there. Perhaps picnic in the post climate of climate change?

Shaddup. Picnic was a finger of speech.

Excuse me. I have authority on picnics. I went on a picnic with a girl once.

Oh, you went on a picnic with a girl. Was she blind in the eyes or what?

Oh no. She had green eyes, liquid green like moss under water. Oh she was a beauty you can believe it. She made devilish eggs, sprinkled red, and there was a bottle of wine too. We sat under a big shade tree on the edge of reality. Oh you could see far and wide in those days. Weren't those the days when you went on a picnic with a girl. And yes a line of ants came down the tree trunk in single file to join our picnic, and the girl said that was all right with her the ants come to the picnic because they are part of everything. And if they are coming all that way we would share. So those ants she served them fried chicken and the devilish eggs and chocolate cake for dessert. I remember, chocolate cake.

Shaddup you idyot. You never knew no girl or had chocolate pie under no tree. Not in this life. Not in no million years.

It doesn't seem like this life any more. I mean, Daddy I didn't know I was happy then but now I see that I was.

I can't stand talk about happiness.

Oh yeah, happy fantasies is the locomotion behine the long slow train.

What the fuck does that mean?

It's a fingering of speech, you wouldn't know.

The short man's arm whips out and strikes the Fat Man in the stomach.

Oovhhh, the Fat Man doubles over, What you'd do that for?

Ignoramus. Now cut me a chew of that bor meat.

You sure about that? What if the owner of this bor comes back and finds us.

Nobody owns nothin. Anyone come here kill'em. Understan?

I gess so. How you know it's bor meat?

Because you're boring me that's why. That

makes everything bor, understand?

Sure I do.

Just do it.

The two men stand next to the fire and chew the meat.

Hmmm. I never did preciate bor befor, if you know what I mean, good.

The little man's arm strikes the big man in the stomach again and this time the big man doubles over and retches.

Stupid. That ain't no bor.

I didna mean to be boring you. I didna mean.

Never mind. Ever thing is boring now. Cut off the meat and put in in the pack and lets get out of here before someone comes.

Maybe they come back with nother bor. We wait and take it.

The boy climbs down out of the tree and stands beside the man and the Woman who are watching the two men from the edge of the forest.

Where the hell did these guys come from? I want jacket like that. I want to kill 'em so I can have it.

The man and the Woman and the boy are invisible to the Fat Man and the thin man who stand on the other side of the fire. Plumes of smoke obscure the two groups.

You can't kill for whatever you want. Besides it's too big for you.

I'll grow into it.

No you won't. The boy turns away and starts to cry.

You didn't have to say that.

Yes I did.

That's my meat, says the boy. He runs around the fire pit.

The small man keeps chewing.

126

That's my meat you're stealing, yells the boy.

The small man coughs. He claps a hand to his mouth to suppress it and when he takes it away blood drips from his hand. The small man looks at his hand. The Fat Man watches, eyes wide and fearful.

He coughs again and red splatters fly out of his mouth.

Daddy don't do that.

Oh. The small man wipes his hand on his sleeve, sags at the knees, drops to the ground.

Oh Daddy... please don't do that.

This is the end for me.

Don't say things like that.

Shut up. It's my time and there's nothing for it. I'm cold.

The Fat Man sobs into the crook of his arm.

Bird and the Woman walk around to the other

side of the fire where the two men are standing.

Build up the fire, says Bird.

They prop the small man on some logs. His breath is a febrile rill. The Woman drips water on his cracked lips. Blood bubbles at his nostrils, and his eyes roll back. The head lolls, the Woman pulls his jacket up and covers him, the wiry body spasms and is still. The Fat Man weeps.

What's the big deal, it's just another dead person, says the boy, ain't you ever seed dead people?

There is sanctity, always, says the Woman.

What am I going to do without my daddy?

Grow up maybe, you tub of lard. I never had no daddy and look at me.

Maybe, says Fat Man, you had a daddy you be nicer.

Fuck you Fat Man. Grow up steal meat like you and your old man here?

I go bury him so the animals don't eat him.

The ground starts shaking again. The Fat Man picks up his daddy but then falls onto one knee. The boy braces himself against a hemlock. The trees shake and crack. The earth opens up and roots crawl out of the ground.

Maybe my daddy lucky one, get out of here first.

It's not going to be a picnic, that's for sure.

I went on a picnic once with a girl.

And the ants came for cake and ice cream.

That's right. And there was a girl there with green eyes.

What the hell is a picnic? says the boy.

I remember a picnic now. A long time ago when I was a little girl. My father carried a basket and mother spread a quilt on the ground.

Oh, says the Fat Man smiling, still down on one knee. I like the sound of that. Then what?

We were beside the ocean. It was blue and so soft

a breeze slid over the warm sand. The air was salty.

Any ants at that picnic?

No everything about that day was perfect.

Really. I wish I was there.

That's a stupid thing to say.

Maybe not.

I too went on a picnic once.

What did you have to eat at your picnic?

The ground shakes, the tree roots climb out of the soil. From the woods the sounds of trees falling, the gathering rustling closing of forest doors.

My favorite was chicken and macaroni with brownies for dessert.

The little dead man flops on the Fat Man's shoulder.

You carry him like a deer   Maybe eat that old man for picnic, eh. Let's put him over the fire.

The Fat Man starts to cry again.

Is that a band?

Cherry pie. Tremors.

It feels warmer.

Lemon meringue pie was my favorite.

That guy is dripping, says the boy. Everyone looks at the stain on the ground. A thread of blood hangs from the little man's mouth.

I'd rather talk about the picnic I went on with a girl.

Yeah, right, and she had purple eyes. Never again my friend, never again.

No, they were green.

That is a band and it's coming closer. I don't know if I can stand another friggin anthem band.

Look, more smoke.

That's the stadium.

Under the orange sky.

It's the big fire.

That old man dripping is grossing me out.

That's more than the stadium on fire.

Yeah it's a big fire.

The Fat Man, the boy, the Woman, and Bird look at the red sky in the west. The air is smudgy and smoky.

That sky looks like a painting. Only it's real, sure it is.

It's red, he says, it's red. He holds up his hand and moves it around in a circle so the group can see.

I just don't know if I want to bury my daddy under the dirt. I don't know.

Daddy ain't goin know. You going carry him around like that forever?

I don't know. Maybe I will.

What are you doing Bird, going somewhere?

Bird slices off chunks of meat and stuffs them in his pockets.

There's nowhere to go. But I'm going.

The boy coughs again and looks at his hand. The Woman moves to his side and puts an arm around his shoulder.

I'm sad, says the Fat Man. I'm sad. He bows his head.

And that stupid old man is still dripping, yells the boy. He releases the Woman's arm and runs toward the Fat Man. Beats the dead man with the stick.

I don't know what to do, the Fat Man sobs. I don't know where to go and I don't know what to do. Daddy's gone and I'm alone.

Big baby, yells the kid. You're a big fucking baby.

Strikes the dead man's head with a stick.

The Fat Man hefts his daddy onto his shoulder. He turns away from the group and shambles down the trail weeping.

I'm sad, I'm sad.

Bird takes the boy by the arm and they disappear into the dark forest of hemlock. The Woman lingers by the fire, leans in and stirs the coals with a stick.

CPSIA information can be obtained
at www.ICGtesting.com
Printed in the USA
LVOW10s1932190417
531397LV00010BA/1121/P

9 780692 725238